THIS WALKER BOOK BELONGS TO:

_____

_____

_____

First published 2006 by Walker Books Ltd   87 Vauxhall Walk, London SE11 5H   This edition published 2007

to be identified as author/illustrator of this work has been asserted by her in accordance with the Copyright, Designs and

Printed in China   All rights reserved.   British Library Cataloguing in Publication Data: a catalogue record for this book is available from the British Library

ISBN: 978-1-4063-0396-4   www.walkerbooks.co.uk

6 8 10 9 7

© 2006 Niamh Sharkey   The right of Niamh Sharkey   This book has been typeset in Sharkey.

Patents Act 1988

For Oscar

I'm a Happy Hugglewug

Niamh Sharkey

WALKER BOOKS
AND SUBSIDIARIES
LONDON · BOSTON · SYDNEY · AUCKLAND

My Hugglewug Song

Oh, oh, oh...
I'm a Hugglewug and I'm happy.
I jump in the air.
I've got twirly whirly horns
and spikey spikey hair.
I wriggle my fingers
and twiddle my toes.
Between my shiny shiny
eyes is my sniffy
sniffy nose.

My mouth is wibbly wobbly.

My tongue is this l... o... n... g...

My Hugglewug Family

My brother Cobby

Baby Ivor's teddy

My baby brother Ivor

My sister Lola

My mummy

My pet fish Horace

Me (Henry)

My daddy

My grandaddy

My nanny

Start the Day the Hugglewug Way!

Baby Ivor loves his porridge.

Gurgle wurgle

I love hugging Mummy.

Lola loves dancing after breakfast.

Cobby and Daddy love reading.

Come and Meet My Hugglewug Friends!

1, 2, 3,
we're off to school!

Hey! There's Oscar
chasing Denzel.
Go, go, guys

I see Mini and Max
on the slide.

Gertie is
skipping.

Bang that drum,
Ruby!

Jump over that
mushroom, Meg!

Splash! Splosh!
Stanley is in a puddle.

It's Time for Hugglewug School!

Here comes a Hugglewug
through the window,

here comes a
Hugglewug through
the door.

Here comes a Hugglewug
round the corner,

Hugglewugs! Hugglewugs! Hugglewugs!
At Hugglewug School we learn to ...

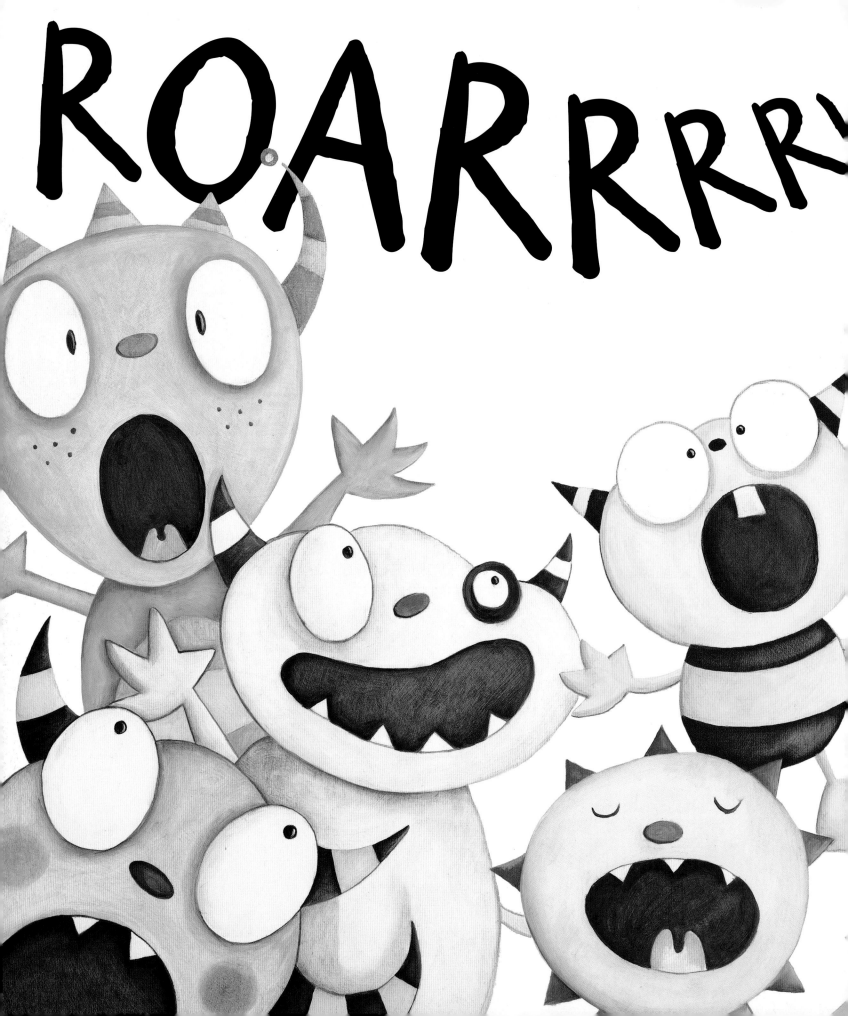

The Scary Hugglewug Counting Game

1 Little

2 Little

4 Little

5 Little

7 Little

8 Little

9 Little Hugglewugs

3 Little Hugglewugs

6 Little Hugglewugs

10 Little Hugglewugs ...

CAN'T SCARE

ME!

Let's All Paint a Picture!

Scribble!

Splosh!

Look! Lola's dancing
with a paintbrush.

Cobby is drawing a
scary blue monster.

Squelch!

Squirt!

Ruby loves being messy.

Careful with
that red paint, Denzel!

What a lovely picture!

Climb the Hugglewug Tree!

It's after school — yippee yippee!
Time to play before our tea.

Whee!

Way hey!

Hugglewugs! Hugglewugs! Up a tree!
How many Hugglewugs can you see?

I Spy Hugglewug Pie

Muffin

Carrot

Hugglewug pie

Apple

Glass of
lemonade

Fork

Knife

Hugglebug

Spoon

Worm

Red
mushroom

Hugglewug
cake

Yellow
mushroom

Snail

Peas

Popcorn

Plate

Our Hugglewug Animal Friends

Woof

Woof

Nibble nibble

There are Lola and Hugglewug dog.

Oink oink

Hugglewug rabbit loves to munch on carrots.

Baby Ivor is playing snap with Hugglewug pig.

Who Loves a Hugglewug?

Mummy
is so
squelchy!

Cobby
is so
huggly!

Daddy
is so
blobby!

My Hugglewug Lullaby

I see the moon,
the moon sees me.

Hugglewug moon!
Hugglewug me!

Let's Sing Again!

Oh, oh, oh...

I'm a Hugglewug
and I'm happy.
I jump
in the air.

I've got twirly whirly horns

and spikey spikey hair.

I wriggle my fingers

and twiddle my toes.

Between my shiny shiny eyes is my sniffy sniffy nose.

My mouth is wibbly wobbly.

My tongue is this l... o... n... g...

S: Come on, everybody! Sing our Hugglewug Song!

Oh, oh, oh...

WALKER BOOKS is the world's leading
independent publisher of children's books.
Working with the best authors and illustrators
we create books for all ages, from babies
to teenagers – books your child will
grow up with and always remember. So…

FOR THE BEST CHILDREN'S BOOKS,
LOOK FOR THE BEAR